OLIVIA
and the Best Teacher Ever

adapted by Ilanit Oliver
based on the screenplay "Teacher of the Year" written by Scott Gray
illustrated by Shane L. Johnson

Simon Spotlight
New York   London   Toronto   Sydney   New Delhi

Based on the TV series *OLIVIA™* as seen on Nickelodeon™

SIMON SPOTLIGHT
An imprint of Simon & Schuster Children's Publishing Division
1230 Avenue of the Americas, New York, New York 10020
Copyright © 2012 Silver Lining Productions Limited (a Chorion company).
All rights reserved. OLIVIA™ and © 2012 Ian Falconer. All rights reserved.
All rights reserved, including the right of reproduction in whole or in part in any form.
SIMON SPOTLIGHT and colophon are registered trademarks of Simon & Schuster, Inc.
For information about special discounts for bulk purchases, please contact Simon & Schuster Special Sales
at 1-866-506-1949 or business@simonandschuster.com.
Manufactured in the United States of America 0412 LAK
1 2 3 4 5 6 7 8 9 10 First Edition
ISBN 978-1-4424-3599-5 (pbk)
ISBN 978-1-4424-5317-3 (eBook)

"Good morning, class!" said Mrs. Hoggenmuller. "I'd like you to welcome someone who is joining us for the day."
Everyone looked up, eager to meet their mystery guest.
"This is Mrs. Stern," Mrs. Hoggenmuller continued.
"Hello, Mrs. Stern," the kids greeted her politely.

"Is she a teacher?" Olivia asked.

"No, Olivia. She's come to watch our class," Mrs. Hoggenmuller explained.

"I'm picking the best teacher to win the city's Teacher of the Year award," Mrs. Stern added seriously, writing something down on her clipboard.

Everyone thought Mrs. Hoggenmuller deserved to win.

"Mrs. Hoggenmuller, what does the teacher of the year get?" Daisy asked.

"Their picture on the side of every school bus in town!" Mrs. Hoggenmuller said cheerfully. "I've always dreamed of being on a school bus!"

Seeing her teacher so excited gave Olivia an idea. She turned to Francine. "I'm going to do whatever it takes to make sure Mrs. Hoggenmuller wins that award!"

"Let's get started, class," Mrs. Hoggenmuller said. "Ni hao, children!"
"Ni hao, Mrs. Hoggenmuller!" the class replied.
"Very good! I see you remember how to say hello in Mandarin Chinese."

Mrs. Stern was very impressed. She smiled as she wrote something on her clipboard. Olivia was pleased. "Mrs. Hoggenmuller is definitely going to win," she whispered to Francine.

Next Mrs. Hoggenmuller assigned the morning chores. It was Olivia's and Daisy's turn to clean the frog terrarium.

"No problem, Mrs. Hoggenmuller!" Olivia told her teacher politely. Then she turned to Daisy. "Whatever it takes to help Mrs. Hoggenmuller win teacher of the year!"

Olivia noticed Mrs. Stern writing on her clipboard. Olivia gave her a nice, big smile before heading toward the terrarium.

Daisy took the lid off the terrarium. "I'll hold Hopper, and you clean," she told Olivia.

But Olivia didn't think that was fair. She wanted to hold Hopper!

"I'm holding that frog!" Daisy protested.

"No, I'm holding that frog!" replied Olivia.

Before they knew it, Hopper hopped right over their heads and out into the classroom. In fact he was headed toward Mrs. Stern!

"Oh no, look!" cried Olivia.

She had to get that frog before he ruined Mrs. Hoggenmuller's chance to become teacher of the year! Olivia grabbed a tall princess hat, and just as Hopper was about to jump on Mrs. Stern's head, Olivia lunged forward and trapped Hopper inside it! Startled, Mrs. Stern turned to find Olivia standing right next to her, wearing the hat!

"Uh, look, I'm a princess!" Olivia said, striking a pose.

"That was close," Olivia told Daisy when she returned to the terrarium. "You hold Hopper. I'll clean."

When Olivia was almost done, Mrs. Hoggenmuller and Mrs. Stern came by to see how they were doing. The terrarium was almost spotless!

"Great terrarium cleaning, girls!" Mrs. Hoggenmuller said.
"Very nice, indeed," agreed Mrs. Stern, writing on her clipboard.
"Mrs. Hoggenmuller's going to win!" Olivia told Daisy. "She's going to get her face on a bus!"

Olivia imagined what it would be like to have her face on something. *"I wonder . . . My face on a bus would be nice!*

Or on a plane! Even better!

Whoa! My face on Mount Rushmore—that's the best yet!"

The sound of Mrs. Hoggenmuller's voice pulled Olivia from her daydream. "It's time for puppet story time," her teacher said.

The class loved puppet story time, and Mrs. Hoggenmuller was telling their favorite story, *Goldilocks and the Three Bears*. Everyone was enjoying it—well, everyone except Mrs. Stern, who let out a big yawn as her head began to droop. Olivia was worried. "Mrs. Stern must be really bored!" she whispered to Francine.

Then Olivia had an idea. "Mrs. Hoggenmuller!" she cried out. "Your story is so exciting. Can I play the bears?"

"Why not!" said Mrs. Hoggenmuller.

Olivia pretended to be the bears as loudly as she could. Instead of just telling the story, she sang a *very* loud song and accompanied herself with a toy drum. Her song was so loud, even Mrs. Stern had to stay awake!

Next it was time for crafts. Everyone loved crafts, especially Olivia!
"Where is the red paint?" Olivia asked Francine.
"Daisy is using it," Francine replied.

Olivia looked over and saw Daisy struggling to get the paint out of the tube. One more squeeze and the red paint would fly through the air and splatter all over Mrs. Stern's clothes!

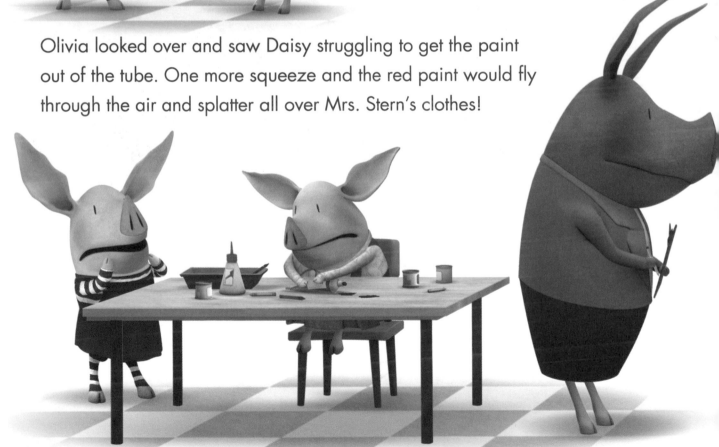

Olivia thought fast. She grabbed a piece of paper and ran to catch Daisy's paint with it, but she accidentally tripped and smashed right into Mrs. Stern! Olivia stopped the red paint from splattering onto Mrs. Stern, but she also made her bump into the frog terrarium, tipping off the lid. Hopper jumped out, right onto Mrs. Stern's head!

Mrs. Stern wasn't used to having a frog on her head. She screamed and ran around the classroom trying to get Hopper off. Finally she landed in a chair, and Hopper hopped off. The entire class thought this was hilarious. But Mrs. Stern did not!

"You can forget about being teacher of the year," she told Mrs. Hoggenmuller. "There's no learning going on in here—just shenanigans!"

And with that, Mrs. Stern left their classroom.

"Oh well," said Mrs. Hoggenmuller sadly, "there's always next year. Okay, it's time for free play outside!"

Mrs. Hoggenmuller tried to put on a brave face, but Olivia could see she was upset.

"It's not fair," Olivia told Francine outside. "Mrs. Hoggenmuller is the best teacher."

"Remember when she taught us the planets by dressing up as them?" Francine said.

"And when she taught us addition and subtraction using apples?" Harold added.

"The planet Neptune is blue," began Francine.

"And one plus one is two!" finished Harold.

"That rhymes, just like a song!" Olivia cried out. Then she had the greatest idea ever!

"Gather round, everyone!" Olivia called to her classmates. "We're going to put on a show to let Mrs. Hoggenmuller know that to us, she's the best teacher ever!"

"Class! It's time to come in!" Mrs. Hoggenmuller called as she stepped outside. But she was surprised to find her class standing in a striking formation.

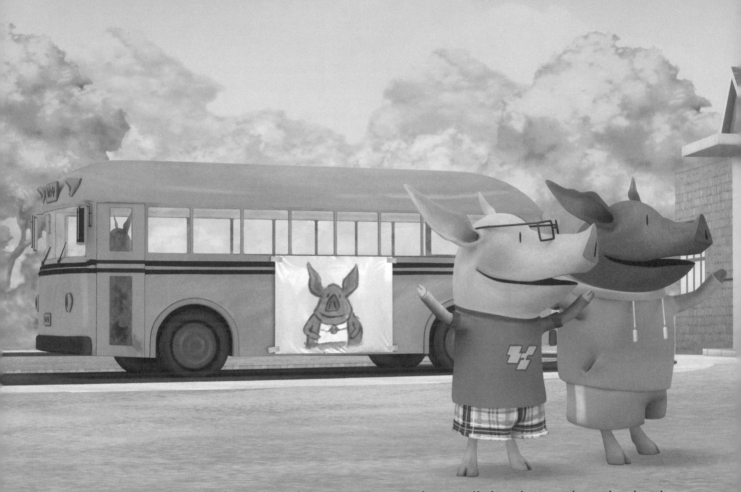

And even more so when they began to sing about all the things that she had taught them: how to count to ten in Mandarin and French, how to construct a sentence, even the fact that camels have humps! When they were done singing, a school bus pulled up with a picture of Mrs. Hoggenmuller hanging on the side.

"Congratulations, Mrs. Hoggenmuller! You're Teacher of the Year!" Olivia announced.

"Thank you, Olivia!" said Mrs. Hoggenmuller. "Thank you, everybody! Let's go for a ride!"

That night Olivia told her mother about the things she had learned from
Mrs. Hoggenmuller.

"Did you know there are three hundred sixty-five days in a year? And flies taste
with their feet?" Olivia asked.

"That's incredible, dear," her mother said. "Do you know how many minutes until
bedtime?"

"Zero?" Olivia replied, fighting off a big yawn.

"That's exactly right," her mom said. "Good night, Olivia."